Sliding into Hell

Sliding into Hell

JOHN BERRY

First published 2005 by
Retro Speedway
Tel: 01708 734 502
Website: www.retro-speedway.com

Printed by Biddles Ltd, King's Lynn, Norfolk

Cover Design:Marios Flourentzou

Distributed by Retro Speedway
103, Douglas Road, Hornchurch, Essex, RM11 1AW
Tel: 01708 734 502
Email: editorial@retro-speedway.com

Set in Times New Roman

ISBN: 0-9551176-0-7

Chapter 1

'Will you lot *please* show some respect! There's a young man *dying* in here!'

Vincent's soul, looking on as an observer, from a position high above the hospital bed, had been upset by the noise and clamour. The discordant sounds had come from somewhere outside of the small room with its single motionless patient, life-preserving equipment, and the ever present Angel in White.

The voice of the Angel, calling from a window overlooking the place where the offending noise had come from, had silenced the intrusion and the room had returned to its normal state of peace and tranquillity.

Perhaps now, Vincent's soul could get back to making the decision it had been putting off for some little time. Which way to go? At one end of the tunnel was a bright, welcoming light. At the other end were nothing but pain and bad things. Vincent's soul had pretty much made the decision to go towards the light. The only thing delaying it was the Angel in White.

The Angel's sweet voice, even raised in anger, as it had been just now, had complicated things with her words. The confused soul had realised the 'dying boy' the Angel had referred to was him, Vincent Hansing.

Stubbornness now kicked in. How dare she say *he* was dying? He was just heading toward the light.

All this effort soon became too much for the young man. For the time being, he would stay where he was, in this warm, fuzzy, dark velvet cocoon, where decisions did not need to be made.

The banging, shouting and clattering had come from several loud, young roughnecks as they had begun to erect scaffolding in preparation for repainting the outside window frames of the eighteenth century-built hospital. To them, this was just another job and just another building.

The austere greystone walls and concrete lintels on the outside contrasted starkly with the warm room, filled, as it was, with so much high-tech equipment. Although even inside in this intensive care unit, reminders of the old-fashioned construction were still obvious. The sash-cord window let in draught, and the high ceilings in such a small room made the dimensions appear all wrong. The people of Shelford had been due a new hospital for some time but, here in 1978, they were still waiting.

Patients who wound up in here were invariably not concerned with the aesthetics of the place, as this particular room, right at the end of the corridor, was merely a holding unit. There was nothing posted on the door, but those who worked in the hospital knew this was merely a grieving place for relatives while they became resigned to the inevitable.

The interruption to the young man's reverie had caused a blip on the screen monitoring his vital signs. Not a big blip, but enough for the owner of the angry voice to notice. She wasn't an angel, but a young nurse in a crisp, white uniform. She had been praying for this blip for almost three weeks.

Initially she had watched and waited because she was being paid to do so. Then, as she had spent all those hours by this young man's side, looking after him, tending to his cleanliness and bodily functions, and monitoring the life-providing mechanical devices, she had become uncomfortably close to the teenager. A teenager she didn't even know.

Alerted by that blip on the screen and the jerk on the graphs monitoring his life forces – the first since her patient had been brought into the special unit and hooked up to the machines, nurse Ann Brown called in the duty houseman.

Little more than a student himself, the young houseman had no idea what the signs were saying. Should he inform the senior registrar or the consultant neurosurgeon?

'Play safe,' he decided. 'Don't want to be seen as a Nervous Nelly'. The machines had settled back down. Surely, to be significant, the reaction would have to appear again and become more obvious?

'I'm sure it was nothing,' the young man said, wishing he had not been called.

Ann disagreed. As a well-trained and instinctive nurse, she had a different opinion. If there was even the remotest chance of kick-starting things, it should be taken. Even though the machines had settled back down, she knew the situation had changed for the better. She was sure there was now a chance, however slim, the young patient might live.

However, she decided to keep her own counsel. All this young intensive care unit nurse would do at this stage was to make even more of a fuss of her patient than she had previously. She spent more time sitting and reading to him and just chatting, as she carried on her duties of checking the various tubes and equipment controlling his life and his destiny.

All this time, the young nurse couldn't work out why she had become so involved. It wasn't as if she hadn't seen her share of trauma and death in this room. She had been on duty when Vincent had been rushed in by ambulance from the speedway track, about a mile away. Head injuries, they had said, and he had been 'dead' for maybe five minutes. The ambulance men had kept lungs working and blood circulating by performing mouth-to-mouth before he had been hooked up to the ventilator in the hospital.

Ann had seen it all before. The parents would be summoned, and the lad would be kept on the life support equipment just long enough to let them come to terms with the fact that he was now merely spare parts. Gone were the days when doctors declared people dead at the scene of an accident. Good organs were hard to come by and nice, healthy young ones were considered a real bonus. It was worth keeping the machines going in the hopes that the parents could be 'educated' into allowing all the undamaged spare parts to be harvested and recycled.

However many times she saw it, Ann could never come to terms with this 'breaker's yard' mentality when dealing with real people. She was not particularly religious, but she felt the medical profession had no right to decide when someone was past trying to save. Nobody, in her view, had the right to say who should live and who should not. She had often wondered in her own mind how many times life-support machines had been turned off prematurely, and, more specifically, for the wrong reasons.

As luck would have it, Vincent had been kept in this state of suspension for much longer than would normally be the case, because his separated parents had been in different parts of the world. Vincent's childhood sweetheart, Dianne, had been with him when he was brought in, had spent the first 48 hours by his side and had done all her grieving by now. She still visited for a while each day to sit holding his hand, but had long since become conditioned to the inevitable.

Many times, she had fantasised that she would have to be the one to make the decision and be responsible for allowing the machines to be turned off, but she was inwardly relieved she would not be given that responsibility.

Vince and her had talked about marriage and if those frequent monthly 'scares' had been any more than that, no doubt the knot between her 18-year-old self and him, only a year older, would have already been tied. Then, turning off the machines would have been *her* decision to make.

As she sat there with time on her hands, Dianne reviewed her life with Vincent. She had been in the year below him at school and she remembered the thrill when she was only 14 and he had asked her out. For the biggest heart-throb in the fourth form to have selected her, a mere third-former, had been a great honour. Even then, Vincent Hansing, with his good looks, ready smile and devil-may-care attitude, had been the one all the other third form girls whispered about as they began the long and winding path through adolescence.

Dianne remembered their first 'date'. He had taken her to the pictures to see *Saturday Night Fever*, and by the end of the evening, she had learned how to 'snog', although he had been a gentleman and not tried anything on. Not on their first date, anyway.

Those were the days. She recalled some of the crazy and dangerous stunts he used to get up to, always taking on challenges, especially involving climbing. He had been the one who had climbed up a drainpipe of their pre-war, two-storey school, then gone up onto the roof and climbed the ornamental look-out tower, before finally shinning up the spire to the very tip and placing a waste-paper basket upside down on the top.

The basket had stayed up there for weeks whilst the authorities worked out how to get it down safely.

She recalled her present to him on his 16th birthday. It had been her virginity. The encounter had only been memorable because it had been the first time, but practice made perfect and they had soon got the procedure down to a fine art.

She also remembered the problem between Vincent's parents, and how, as a result, he had eventually been forced to live in the spare room at her parents' house.

Dianne had grown into a willowy beauty with dark, wavy hair and the most striking of green eyes. Although she had never fully allowed herself to see it, by the time the young lady had left school, she was considered every boy's ultimate desire. Dianne and Vincent had been Shelford Central School's perfect couple.

Chapter 2

The injured rider's parents were temporarily reunited over his hospital bed the day after the scaffolders had arrived and nearly a week after his admission. It was no happy reunion though. One agreed to the equipment being turned off and the young man's body parts being used elsewhere but the other did not.

The hospital authorities assumed the longer things went on, the more likely it would be that the father would ultimately change his mind and remove his objection. Another few days for him to come to terms with his son's death should do it. This wearing down process was almost routine.

The next day there was an ugly confrontation between the parents. It began when Vincent's father, Charlie, arrived at the hospital to find his ex-wife, Iris, discussing the boy's funeral arrangements with Dianne. Charlie overreacted and a row broke out.

When Charlie had seen his ex for the first time in nearly four years, it was all he could do to stop himself from bursting out laughing. Given any other scenario and he would not have tried to contain himself. Now in her fortieth year, and showing it, she obviously imagined herself as 25. She still sported peroxide hair, red lipstick and a short skirt. Charlie had taken one glance and thought to himself: 'My God, it's Patsy Stone's younger sister!'

Ann Brown, the on-duty intensive care unit nurse, busied herself with performing routine duties but remained within earshot. She just could not believe how these three people were discussing the funeral arrangements at all, let alone in such a loud and angry way. Not only were they arguing over whether Vincent should be buried or cremated, and where his body should be laid to rest, but they also continued to debate the 'harvesting' of his body parts, whilst he lay there directly under their noses.

It seemed to Ann the two women were wearing Charlie down and he was getting ready to give in, so she carefully positioned herself between the bed and the door. As she had suspected, Charlie was on the point of cracking.

'Oh, please yourselves,' he yelled, as he stormed out of the tiny room.

Ann followed. Charlie stood there in the bleak and unforgiving corridor, head in hands wanting to scream but knowing it would not help. The girl timidly touched this angry and frustrated man's arm and asked for a word. Gently, and very carefully, she posed the possibility that Vincent might not actually be beyond saving.

It was not for her to tell Charlie that the senior hospital consultants had written off his son long ago or that effectively, he had been filed away to wait recycling. Nor would it have been ethical or fair to tell him about the tiny– but to her mind, significant – reaction she had seen just two days previously. She was brave enough, however, to suggest the father speak with the hospital administration to ask them if he could have the case reviewed, and maybe have some independent opinion sought.

Now you don't challenge senior hospital consultants easily. Many in the medical profession would prefer to bury their mistakes rather than admit they could have been wrong, and the whole system has always been geared to closing ranks. Charlie Hansing knew he would not have an easy time of it. He was just a normal run-of-the-mill kind of guy. Some might even say he was one of life's losers. Certainly, he was anything but a crusader.

This had been the first time since the crash at the speedway, though, that anyone at all had said something positive and Charlie duly grasped the opportunity to do something constructive. It surely had to be better than arguing with his ex-wife about funeral arrangements.

Possibly, had he rationalised it, he would have accepted that he was merely trying to make up for not having been there supporting his son on that fateful night . . . and on the many other nights when Vincent could have done with a bit of parental input but had missed out because of Charlie's constant feuding with Iris.

This was a chance, small though it was, to give Vincent something back. In the meantime, if the delay caused by stirring things up at the hospital frustrated Iris, then so much the better.

The sad thing was, Vince had somehow heard and followed the row going on over his head in the single bed ward, albeit from a long way away. Deep in the inner reaches of his mind the words 'suit yourself' had nestled. He was not aware of his father's determination to go and bat for him.

Charlie was just an ordinary bloke. He could sit inconspicuously on a London Underground train, reading *The Sun*, and not ever be subjected to the stares of other passengers as they scanned the carriage for interesting faces to relieve their boredom. He would have made the perfect private detective. Nobody would ever have bothered to give him a second look. It would not be an easy thing for him to stir things up with the hospital authorities but he knew he had to rise above his normal desire to avoid confrontation.

Whilst Charlie was rattling on doors and battling, Quixote-style, against the impenetrable closed-ranks of the medical self-protection mechanism, Ann was spending more and more time in room L4 where Vincent remained suspended between the worlds of the living and the dead.

The dedicated young nurse had never enjoyed too much of a social life and the off-duty time she would normally have spent in the nurses' living quarters she now spent with Vincent. Not in civvies, but in uniform, so that, should visitors arrive, she could fade into the background, fiddling with the equipment or generally busying herself. This young girl had added the role of chief protector to her many other duties.

Not that there were that many visitors to Vincent's bedside by now. Speedway fans and casual friends had not been allowed into the ward from the start. Sadly, those who were allowed to visit, even members of his close family and his girlfriend, Dianne, were reduced to just 'looking in' on the young man.

The novelty had worn off. Charlie's stirring up of the hospital complaints system was merely delaying the inevitable, making the visits even more painful. Even those close visitors were all beginning to reach the end of their collective tethers.

Not so with Ann. The longer time went on, the more convinced she was that Vince would pull through. He became her very own living doll. Only children, such as Ann, sometimes invented an invisible 'friend' to play with. That had never happened to her when she was young, but an outsider might well have reached the conclusion that Vincent had now become that 'friend'.

Apart from talking to the comatose patient about nothing in particular, she would also spend hours reading to him, mainly from the newspapers. Often she would begin an article by suggesting he should wake up and take a look at a picture, or maybe she would ask him to look at a cartoon.

Sometimes, when she was tending him, she would give him a

peck on the cheek. Other times, when she was sure nobody was about, she would give him a full kiss on the lips, and whilst washing him or sorting out the catheter, she would gently cradle his testicles in her soft hand. This wasn't a shallow sexual thing, but merely a sign of love. Unhealthy love, perhaps, but love nonetheless.

Ten days had passed since Charlie had begun to rock the hospital boat. Very little of the resultant activity had involved Vincent directly. After all, the medical experts had passed their judgements and were not used to having them queried. They were decidedly unhappy at having their medical expertise questioned, and were certainly most put out to find themselves subjected to the slow, grinding steps of a complaints procedure.

Had they known a mere nurse had generated the whole affair, they would have been mortified.

During all of the weeks Vincent had been lying in this small, quiet room, his soul had been awakened briefly, here and there. It had noted the care of the Angel. It had also noted the comings and goings of the other people. It had seen Dianne sitting crying, and it had witnessed the arguments between parents.

In all this time, though, it still hadn't made a decision about which direction to travel along the warm fuzzy tunnel. Was it to be the light or the pain?

This time the blip on the screen was louder and longer. No, it wasn't as the result of a kiss from Ann. Surely that only happens in fairy stories? This was just the opposite. Once again, Ann had been busying herself bed-bathing the speedway rider when a metal bowl had fallen onto the vinyl floor and shattered the peace. Such an intrusion into Vincent's soft, warm world was unacceptable, and he reacted angrily.

Where was the Angel's voice? Who dared to disturb my tranquillity? Don't they know there's a boy dying here? Who has sent this cacophony of noise? Could it be the Devil's tuneless trumpeters come to do battle with the angel for my soul?

Vincent's reaction had registered on the machines, merely as a series of blips. The regular thump and wheeze of the heart and lung machine altered not a jot, but Ann's own heart went into overdrive! She stared at Vincent's face. Had she seen a slight movement under the eyelids or was this just wishful thinking? She leaned to within an inch or two of his face.

'Vincent, my love, I need you here with me. Time to wake up, my darling. Please, for me?'

No reaction, so she picked up the bowl and deliberately threw it onto the floor again.

Now Vincent was really angry. How dare his perfect world of warmth and comfort be invaded once more? What does the Angel mean, 'time to wake up'? Was she losing the battle with the Devil? Does she need my help?

Again, Vincent's thought patterns registered merely as a series of blips on the screen and jerks on the tracing arm of the graph searching for any brain activity.

Yes! There it was. The eyelids fluttered. They didn't open, but they did most definitely flutter.

If Vincent was angry, Ann was ecstatic! She didn't even bother with the houseman but called for the duty registrar instead. Same bowl, same noise, same reaction.

Vincent was alive!

This time, though, Vincent finally decided the Angel was losing the fight and needed his help. When it had been just himself and the Angel and the warmth and comfort, he had been happy to stay where he was. But because of this invasion, he would have to fight. He was not prepared to see his devoted Angel beaten by the Devil, masquerading in a white coat. This time Vincent's eyes part-opened for a fraction of a second and his heart and lungs began to override the machine.

Ann tried to hide it, but tears just cascaded from her shining eyes down her face, to the biggest grin anyone had ever seen her give.

Chapter 3

The long and winding road back to the land of the living was not filled with fun. The tests, the experimenting, the skull-drilling and the pain were no picnic whatsoever.

Then came the biggest blow of all. Because Vincent had been consigned so early to the breaker's yard, nobody at Shelford General had bothered too much with the other bumps and bruises sustained in the horrific incident. At each of the medical points of call after the crash . . . the Shelford Racers' speedway track, the casualty department and the intensive care unit, all of the interest had been centred on the head, the brain and the ventilator.

What had been no more than a tiny shard of damaged vertebra in his spine had lodged against a nerve. A minor operation would have released the pressure but it had gone unnoticed, and during the weeks of bed-bathing and being turned by the nurses to prevent the formation of bedsores, the shard of bone had effectively sawn through that nerve. By the time anyone had noticed it, the damage had become permanent and irreversible.

For Vincent, the good news was, he was alive. The bad news was, he couldn't walk, had no control over his expelling of waste, and his mighty successful but now very short sex life was also at an end. For this virile, active young man, the good news of his being alive was also the bad news.

Shortly after his move from Shelford General to the specialist spinal damage hospital at Stoke Mandeville, Vincent decided to call it a day. He saw no future in carrying on.

Luckily for him, the staff at that world famous facility were highly qualified to deal with this kind of reaction, which was not uncommon. However, Vincent remained in a bad way, mentally, made even worse by the relaxation of the restriction on visitors compared to Shelford General.

He could not recall the crash at the Shelford Racers' home track that had caused the injuries and little had been said about the incident up until then.

Vince knew Jeff Harding, his team-mate, had been involved. Jeff must have felt bad, because he had been one of the first 'outsiders' to visit him in Shelford General and now here at Stoke Mandeville. Jeff lived quite near to Dianne and several times had kindly brought her down to the hospital from her Midlands home.

Over the first couple of weeks of Vincent's rehabilitation Jeff had, in fact, become something of a regular visitor. This, in itself, was unusual. The pair of riders did not get on that well. Vincent had always been upfront and outgoing whereas Jeff always appeared far more calculating and aloof.

Several of the Shelford supporters also visited their hero at the rehabilitation facility and they could not help but want to talk about the injuries and the terrible crash that had caused them. By then, Vince had also become curious as to what exactly had happened but he was still deeply depressed and unable to cope with the appalling reality of the situation.

The fans had described in detail how Vincent and Jeff Harding had been paired together in the last heat of the match. Harding had made his normal electric start from the inside gate position and Vincent, as he had done so many times, had taken the high, wide, and handsome line around the outside in the first turn.

As he had done so many times, Vincent, perilously close to the fence, had made to come up outside and level with his partner so that they could team-ride home together for a maximum heat win.

This time though, Harding, for some reason nobody could understand, had changed his line on the exit to the turn, when both riders were accelerating hard. He had taken Vincent's front wheel away with his rear tyre, causing the shocked rider to flip over the front of his collapsing bike.

Man and bike had hit the inadequate chain link fence in a terrible smash. It was not clear if Vincent's head had hit a metal fence post, or if it had been his bike that had caused the damage, as both had become entangled together.

All the angry, young man registered from the supporters' gossip at the time was that Jeff Harding had been to blame for the crash. No wonder the bloke was so keen to visit, he thought to himself.

Ann Brown, the nurse to whom Vincent owed his life, was also making regular trips to see him. As soon as the Shelford Racers' star rider had surfaced from his coma, she had covered up her personal feelings, and he had recalled little of her vigil. He put her visits to the Stoke spinal unit down simply to her maybe being a speedway fan and to the way they had got on after he had regained consciousness.

Ann seemed to be the only one who hadn't polarised, like the rest, into either the 'come on, snap out of it' brigade, or the 'there, there' set. Vince didn't know which of those groups he despised more.

As he was being gently weaned off the heavy drugs he had been on, Vince began to have nightmares. Well, not nightmares so much, as disconcerting dreams. Most of these would vanish in the morning light but he did recall glimpses of those dreams: like parents and girlfriend planning funerals, and clattering bowls, and an angel stealing kisses in the night…

What should have been the final hammer blow for Vincent was, in fact, the turning point in his recovery. Dianne arrived one day. Nobody else was about and she sat on the edge of the bed holding his hand, but with a very serious expression on her face. Slowly, she began to explain why.

First, the teenage girl admitted that she just could not come to terms with devoting the rest of her life to a cripple. She had tried very hard, but the terms of engagement between them had changed. Quite apart from the physical side of things, Vince had also changed. He was no longer the fun-loving, dynamic, powerful personality he had been before the crash. Things could never be the same between them.

At that stage, full of tears, Dianne went outside to compose herself, returning hand-in-hand with Jeff Harding. Now Shelford's unrivalled number one rider, the dark haired handsome young man looked sheepish but somehow triumphant.

Dianne was clearly having difficulty coping. So much so, that it was left for Jeff to explain. It seemed he and Dianne had been consoling each other on the journeys to and from the Shelford hospital and then the longer trips to Stoke.

One thing had led to another and Dianne had become pregnant. Dianne and Jeff were to be married as soon as they could. Out of courtesy to Vincent, they had felt they should tell him themselves, rather than let him find out about it from others.

Fight or flee? Fight or flee? Which way would Vincent Hansing go? Would he find a way to end his life or not?

For the second time since his accident, he decided to fight. This time, though, it wasn't his soul making the decision but his heart and mind.

He made a vow that night. People were going to pay for what had happened to him.

Vince had already been through the classic 'why me' bit. To say he had come to terms with the situation would be a massive overstatement but at least he no longer considered himself a lost cause. The feeling sorry for himself phase had turned into pure anger. This wasn't a shouting sulking, fit of tantrums but a much more menacing and dangerous bitterness.

From a room further along the corridor, he could just make out the sound of the radio emitting fading strains of the Chicago saying what would happen *If You Leave Me Now*.

Vincent was not amused. His decision was made. As he closed his eyes, he muttered this oath.

'Fuck that rubbish, fuck *Him*, fuck *Her*. I'll show the lot of them. They will *all* pay.'

It was no idle threat.

He became the model patient. The young man carried out every exercise to the letter. In fact, he begged his physiotherapists to push him harder and harder. He was determined, in the first instance, to get himself walking again.

When he wasn't exercising, he was reading - not short stories or magazines either. He wanted to learn from other victims who had undergone similar experiences.

The people at the hospital were well trained in treading a careful line between optimism and realism. They didn't speak in terms of miracle cures, but they did encourage positive thinking and the advantage of fitness.

Vincent learned fast. Early on in his life, he had been an outstanding student at school. This had not lasted, as much because of his unsettled home environment as anything else. He had played up, got himself a bad reputation and had finally rejected an academic career in favour of becoming a speedway rider.

Reading from medical books as he lay there in hospital, the young man discovered the basic facts about his injury. Nerves cannot be stitched back together like skin, muscle and arteries. Nerves do not rejoin themselves either. Well, not to any significant degree anyway. He learned about stem cell research – then, in the late 70s, in its infancy – and he knew that any positive outcomes were too far away for him to benefit from.

He discovered that a good percentage of people with similar injuries to his could eventually get themselves mobile again, albeit with callipers and sticks, but the important bits, the control of expelling waste, and the pleasure of normal sex, were gone. Vince was consigned to spending his life unable to control his bodily functions, and good, old-fashioned sex was now nothing more than a memory.

Whenever he let his mind stray to such thoughts and from there begin lapsing into self-pity, the one phrase always managed to pull him back: 'Don't get mad, get even.'

Chapter 4

Vincent Hansing's time at Stoke Mandeville wasn't wasted by any means, just the opposite really. His father, Charlie had gone back to salvage his little café/bar in Spain. The five weeks Charlie had spent in England had seen his Costa del Sol business plummet as the local staff had taken all kinds of liberties.

 Much as he loved his son, his father had done all he could for him and just sitting by a bed all day was not going to bring back the use of Vincent's legs. Charlie reasoned that if he could get back to Spain and rebuild the business, at least he could possibly be able to assist financially.

Iris, on the other hand, had flown back to her new husband and lifestyle in America just as soon as Vincent had emerged from his coma. Iris had been the one who had originally left Charlie and the 15-year-old Vincent to fend for themselves nearly four years ago. At that time, she had run off to California with an American air force officer, although it wasn't him who she eventually married, after the divorce from Charlie had finally come through.

Iris had always been a bit flighty and her marriage to Charlie always stormy. Vincent had managed to keep the majority of his thoughts about his mother to himself as he was growing up but had not been heartbroken when she finally left home. His mum had definitely not been the classic cuddly earth-mother type, and just as he was not unhappy when she left the first time, he was equally as dismissive when she went back to America long before he had been transferred to Stoke Mandeville.

Vincent decided he would manage in future without either of his parents. Letters from Charlie, some containing money, remained unopened and unanswered. Iris never even bothered to write.

Moving in with Dianne's family had been a good option when he had turned down his dad's offer to go with him to Spain, nearly two years ago. Even then, at just 17-years old, he had decided he wanted to become the speedway World Champion and over that period had shown all the signs that he might even have made it to the very top. But that was before the crash.

Once he had reconciled himself to the fact that riding speedway was now an impossible dream, Vincent decided he would make himself a plan. Clearly, going back to live at Dianne's parents' house was not an option. His 'adopted' parents had come to visit a few times but he had been unreceptive enough for them to decide it was best to stop.

His only real friend appeared to be Ann. Even though he treated her with disdain, she kept coming back for more. In fact, the greater his efforts were to push her away, the stronger her desire to stay.

During the long, boring hours and days when Ann couldn't get down to visit him, Vincent spent the time with his head in books, Those dealing with his current medical condition and likely outcomes had long since been devoured and notes made and kept, some in the brain and others filed more conventionally. Those involving the law on liability were a little more complex, especially where personal injury was concerned. If he had lived and been injured in America things would have been more clear-cut but, in England, the burden of proving negligence in personal injury cases was much more onerous and the potential payouts far less.

Even so, Vincent maintained his bitter determination. Somebody was going to pay for what had happened to him. It helped his demeanour none when he discovered the paltry limits of the insurance payout from the premiums automatically deducted per race from his weekly pay-cheque.

Twenty-seven pounds and fifty pence a week was the payment, and then only for a maximum of one year. A thousand pounds for permanent loss of use of a limb or an eye and just five thousand pounds for becoming wheelchair-bound. That was how much the speedway authorities thought he was worth.

True, he had signed his annual riding contract, but without having read the four pages of small print. Had he done so, he would have noticed he had signed away his right to hold anyone in speedway liable for anything that had happened to him. However, he did his homework thoroughly and soon discovered the contract he had signed was worth nothing if he had either not understood what he was signing, or if the terms of that contract were manifestly unfair.

Time after time, whenever the tears came close, whenever he woke to face another day, or just before falling asleep after a day filled with despair, he repeated what had now become his all-consuming mantra. *Someone* was going to pay.

Ann's visits were the only time he felt anything positive at all. She was the loyalist of lap dogs. He could do or say anything he wanted to her and she just took it. Sometimes her eyes would well up and give her feelings away and other times Vince sensed the hurt he was causing and backed off a bit. But she never broke down - well, not in front of Vince anyway, and she never offered less than complete support. It was as if her whole life had been assigned to the duty of being Vincent's guardian angel.

Ann had never really been the traditional creature of the 70s. No sex and drugs or rock and roll had come her way. For as far back as she could ever recall, nursing had been her chosen path. There was little doubt she could easily have become a doctor. She had the ability and, certainly, the dedication but her parents had not been able to support her through the years of training, and so she had settled for nursing.

No mini-skirts or mad student parties for her, though. She just had a desire and the determination to get into nursing as soon as possible. Normally it was unheard of for an under 20-year-old to be working in ICU, but Ann's rise in nursing had been meteoric.

So her unqualified good looks, with heart-shaped face and jet-black straight hair, the beautiful porcelain-like smooth white skin, light blue eyes and a body to die for, had never ever been exploited. From tiny terraced house, on to residential nursing school, and finally in hospital nurses' quarters, she stayed with her books and her thoughts whilst the other girls were painting the town.

Even from her early teenage years, Ann had worn National Health glasses. Her sight was not that bad, but she used those glasses as a shield to deflect men. With the plain and simple glasses, a rather severe dress sense and an almost paranoid refusal to make eye contact with the opposite sex, unless they were sick or infirm, she had managed to keep the social niceties at bay.

When the adolescent Ann had been just 14, the 15-year-old boy from across the road had tried to date her. She often recalled how, during the school holidays, she had kissed and cuddled with him and he had touched her breasts. The effect had been electrifying. Her body had simply gone into overdrive and it had frightened her to find she had been close to losing control of herself.

From that time on, any sexual gratification had been self-administered behind locked doors. She was terrified of what it did to her and the danger of losing control of situations with men due to her overactive libido.

Vincent finally finished his hit list. According to him, these were the bodies responsible for his situation, and they would have to be punished.

He started at the scene of the crime, and the primary guilty party, Jeff Harding.

By now Vince had completely unravelled the 'accident' and what had led up to it. He and Jeff had started speedway at the same time, both as 16-year-old kids with Shelford Racers. They had soon stood out as potential champions but Vince had always caught the public eye a little more. He was patently good-looking, with a strong jaw-line and mop of wavy, strawberry-blond hair that both mothers and daughters wanted to tousle.

On a speedway bike, he was the cavalier. He was the one who threw caution to the wind, often putting himself into dangerous situations, but making masses of friends and fans with his guts and style.

Jeff Harding had always been the quiet achiever. Slim, with dark hair, he had carried a swagger and superior air about him all his life. Impeccable equipment and a good gating style saw him, more often than not, into the first turn in front of the three other riders. From there, he could dictate races and was ruthless with anyone who tried to pass.

Even when he didn't reach the first turn in front, he had such a reputation for being a hard nut, other riders were nervous of him and he could normally muscle them out of the way.

The one person Jeff could never intimidate was his own team mate, Vincent Hansing. Whenever they had raced against each other, Vince would somehow always know where Jeff would try to block him, and would buzz by on the other side.

On the surface, they were colleagues and friends but, deep down, Jeff hated the debonair Vincent, with his good looks and his charisma. Then there was Dianne, whom Jeff had always wanted but Vincent had a prior claim to.

On the evening of the crash, Jeff had been told he was to be transferred away from the Shelford team. The promoter, Cyril Grant, said he could not afford to keep both the two stars and he had decided Jeff was the one who would have to go.

That was it. An incensed Jeff had deliberately and calculatingly ridden Vincent into the fence with the sole object of causing injury.

He had succeeded to devastating effect.

These things are always brushed off as 'racing incidents' but Jeff had made a bad mistake. He had been so wound up about the situation, he had told his mechanic before the race what he was going to do. Not long after Jeff and Dianne had been married, the word had got back to Vincent that the crash had been no accident.

Jeff Harding was the villain and number one on Vincent's list, but for the time being there was little to be done. This particular piece of vengeance would have to wait.

Vincent was also told, in great detail, how the duty doctor at the speedway that night had been drinking in the bar all evening. The St John Ambulance people had panicked at the scene. With no medical supervision, they had stood around not daring to touch the badly injured rider, who had lain there motionless for two or three life-ebbing minutes.

It had been Vincent's team mates who had taken matters into their own hands and lifted him into the ambulance without worrying about possible consequential damage.

Vince decided to forgive the St John's people and the other riders. The former should not have been left without medical supervision and the latter at least realised speed at that time was of the essence.

But where was that medical supervision they should have had? The track doctor was in the bar, of course. Everyone knew he was drunk but proving it would be an impossible thing to do. Even proving he had deserted his post would be difficult. All that was required of him according to the regulations was that he be 'in attendance' at the meeting.

Next, Vincent turned his attention to the speedway authorities. Twenty-seven pounds fifty pence a week for one year? They had to be joking. However, the authorities had covered their backs well and legal action against them was not an option.

When it came down to possible compensation, Vincent was left with just the hospital and its doctors to pursue. Even with all the attempted cover-ups, it was clear there had been a lack of proper medical care, resulting in the paraplegia. The liability was clear for all to see. No doubt, each medico would be keen to pass the buck along the line, and so they did, but sooner or later, a clear case of negligence existed.

In his own mind, Vincent could have come to terms with the human error of not diagnosing his broken back. What he would never forgive, although it was never admitted officially, was the manner in which his body had been callously earmarked as spare parts for other people long before all the medical life-saving alternatives had been explored.

Four months after the accident Vince was able to get himself around quite well. The constant physiotherapy had significantly strengthened his upper body and with the help of a hoist over the bed, he could easily get from bed to wheelchair and back again. He failed in his attempts at walking though. With callipers and sticks, he could support himself but he couldn't walk without considerable assistance.

This was another huge disappointment to him but, by that time, he had learned to cope reasonably well both mentally and physically. He was desperate to try and be independent despite being wheelchair-bound. It was a matter of pride.

Soon he would need to face the realities of having to cope on his own. The Shelford supporters had undertaken a collection for him, which had paid for a wheelchair, but he needed funds, and lots of them, to pay for the court case he was determined to take out against the hospital.

Ann was aware of his plan to sue the hospital. She also knew just how much the whole process would cost. The brave girl had made a decision months ago. Now was the time to tell Vince. He and she would have to move in together.

Vince would receive government financial assistance as far as maintaining a basic level of subsistence was concerned, but little more. On his own, he had no hope of funding legal action. If Ann moved in with him, though, and received payments as his primary carer, whilst also working nights in the private nursing system, then she would earn quite good money. They could use Vincent's allowances to live on and save her pay to fund the case.

She suspected what Vincent's first reaction to her plan would be, and so left it until she was about to leave the hospital one day, shortly after he had been told he would soon be released. As she stood up to go, she dropped it on him.

'Oh, by the way, I've been doing some research on purpose-built council accommodation and the various entitlements you are able to claim. It seems to me that two can live as cheaply as one, so I'm going to move in with you as your carer, and we will pool our funds.'

True to form, Vincent's pride jumped to the fore. He ranted about not being a charity case or a kept man. Ann just smiled sweetly, told him to think about the logic of it, and slipped away.

Vincent did think about it. In fact, he thought of very little else. He began to fully realise what Ann meant to him. She was more than just a friend. She was the *only* person in his life. Without her patience, good humour and constant support his existence would really have no purpose other than pure revenge. He had understood for some time how she felt about him but had refused to allow himself to dwell on it. In between feeling sorry for himself and being angry with The World, he had not allowed sentiment to creep in and complicate things.

But he now had to face up to reality. Not just of having to cope with maintaining his existence, but of having a reason for doing so. He considered what life would be like without his angel, but not for too long. The alternative was terrifying.

Ann was off-duty the following day. She dashed around during the morning so that she could get down to Stoke for early afternoon. Vincent had made a real effort. He had showered and washed his hair and was sitting in his wheelchair reading when she came in.

More than usual that day, Ann looked a million dollars in her crisp, white cotton long-sleeved blouse and navy-blue skirt. Her thick black hair was, as always, in a perfect bob, and there was just a hint of pink lipstick and eye make-up. The clothes were anything but sexy but with the sun behind her, Vincent could see the outline of her breasts through the material. For the first time since the accident, he looked at Ann in a way different from that of her being just his nurse and friend.

'Well,' she said, referring to the conversation of the day before. 'Deal?'

By way of reply, Vincent beckoned her nearer. When she was within range, he caught her elbow and gently moved her nearer to his space, running his hand up her arm and tugging her warm body down with gentle pressure.

As she stooped, his hand moved up from arm to shoulder and along to her neck. Now, he drew her head down and kissed her lightly and gently on the lips. It was not a kiss of passion but more than a kiss of friendship. Lips were apart but mouths were not open. It was almost a butterfly's touch, but the hand on the back of the neck was firm.

After a full five seconds, he released his hand. Both of them moved their lips enough to signify mutual happiness, before she drew back.

Ann was red and flushed. Her heart thumped and she felt dizzy. Vincent's breath was also fast and tight. Without saying a word, Ann slid the curtains around, sat on the empty bed, undid the top three buttons on her blouse and put Vincent's hand inside. She bent towards him and this time they kissed as lovers do.

This was her first-ever adult kiss, unlike the fumblings of that adolescent boy from her youth. She had often wondered how it would be but she had never considered just a kiss would have so much power. Fireworks went off in her mind and her body came alive. No amount of self-gratification could possibly compare with this moment.

But moment was all it was. It lasted maybe 20 seconds before Vincent allowed himself to notice two things. The first was the explosive forces he had released in the demure 19-year old in front of him.

Given any other situation, he would have been over the moon. He had also noticed, however, that despite having also experienced a burst of adrenalin enough to register on the Richter scale himself, the thing down below remained entirely dormant, wrapped as it was in its rubber sheath.

The enormity of the situation burst onto him. He was no longer a 'complete' person. Roughly, he dragged his hand away, yanked back the curtain enough to get the wheelchair through, and was gone down the centre of the ward and out of sight.

Ann's flush subsided almost as rapidly as it had arrived but was immediately followed by a panic attack. How can two almost identical physiological functions produce such totally different reactions? Her face, only seconds ago, pink and flushed, was now ashen white.

She re-buttoned her blouse and waited. In the space of just one minute, she had experienced the highest high of her 19-year-old life and then the lowest low. Even though she had been able to cope with all of Vincent's mood swings and self-centred behaviour up until now, this was something different. This was rejection.

About 15 minutes later, one of the ward cleaners found her still sitting on the side of the empty bed with the curtains half pulled back. This was not the first time the woman had seen tears in that place. She knew to listen and comfort but not to press, and Ann was saying nothing. The middle-aged lady took the emotional girl down to the staff area for the elixir of healing – a nice cup of tea.

Chapter 5

Vincent telephoned Ann in the early evening, soon after he calculated she would have arrived back at the nurses' home.

Holding a personal conversation using the pay phone in the corridor outside her ground floor room was never easy. Nurses walking past or chatting in nearby rooms did not deliberately eavesdrop, but just trying to hold a conversation in such a public place was always difficult. It was worse for one so recently bruised. Similarly, Vincent was restricted to using a pay-phone on a trolley in his open ward.

'I didn't mean to upset you,' he said sheepishly. 'I was being selfish and insensitive as usual.'

'I thought I must have done something wrong?' was all she could think to say in reply.

'Just the opposite. I simply could not handle my - incapacity.' He was trying to find the right words to show his inner feelings but they just wouldn't come. He had forgotten how to be tender and even how to show affection.

'I do want us to live together. I think it is a wonderful idea...'

Ann made it as easy as she could by trying to be positive and talk of practical things but the conversation was always going to be stilted, with lots of pauses. Finally came the pips from the mobile public telephone in the ward. Ten seconds to put more money in or be cut off.

'No more change,' he lied.

'But I *do* love you.'

The line cut out. Ann put the receiver down and quickly disappeared back into the privacy of her own tiny room, weeping again, as she had been doing for much of the day. This time, though, the tears were warm, not cold. She lay on her bed, felt for her private area and thought of that kiss.

So much to do and so little time, Ann had just three weeks in which to make all the arrangements in time for her man's release.

Vincent made plenty of phone calls and filled in the seemingly hundreds of forms, and as luck would have it the local council found him a place.

It was a tiny, one-bedroom, purpose-built, wheelchair-friendly unit in the small east Midlands town of Kreswick. This was nowhere near where either of them had lived before, but they weren't bothered. It was close to shops, services and a decent medical group practice.

It had taken a little time to get over the embarrassment of The Kiss. On her next visit to Stoke Mandeville, Ann had walked straight up to Vincent and given him a peck on the mouth. This had broken the ice but it was not until the council unit had been offered that they actually got around to discussing things of a personal nature.

The unit had just the one bedroom, along with a living area incorporating a kitchenette. There was also a bathroom purpose built for wheelchair-bound people. Vincent would need a hospital-style bed and hoist in order to get in and out of his bed easily, so Ann suggested she would sleep in the living room on a divan couch.

'Don't you want to sleep with me, then?' was Vincent's response to her idea.

'Of course,' she said, colouring up, 'but I didn't want to upset you again.'

At last, the subject had been raised. Vincent took her hand. He had been rehearsing this speech for quite some time.

'We both know I am now impotent. As a nurse, you understand this and all the implications. You still come to see me and you want to live with me, so I presume you have thought things through and are still prepared to stay with the cripple that I am.

'I cannot give you what you have had from others. I know this is unreasonable on you, and I vow to try to solve the problem somehow.'

Once again, the tears were close for both of them.

'I don't think you realise,' she said quietly. 'I've never been touched by any man before, so I have nothing to miss. It will be no problem at all for me.'

Vincent pondered for a moment. He hadn't bargained for this. On the one hand, it made things easier in that she would not be constantly thinking of former lovers. But on the other hand, it was not at all fair that she should be expected to go through life as a virgin.

He realised that particular avenue of conversation was too difficult. Now was not the time to talk of such things. He decided to change direction.

'This is the sleeping arrangement I had in mind,' he ventured.

'Assuming there is enough space, we can arrange for a normal single bed to go alongside the hospital-style one I need. We can either search around for an old fashioned, tall iron bedstead or we can get a modern bed and put it on blocks so the two beds will be the same height. If we then use king-sized bed linen, effectively we will be sleeping together.'

Ann readily agreed, and she searched the second-hand furniture shops during the next week, for an old fashioned bedstead, but in the end they settled for a raised divan.

By the time Vincent was released from hospital, the tiny unit had been furnished with all the basic necessities of life and the various government agencies provided enough ongoing money for the pair of them to exist on.

The trip up to their new home in the hospital car was harrowing for Vince. He hadn't realised how difficult it would be to confront the outside world face to face again. It should have been a day to remember but it was daunting, and he was glad they could go straight to their new home without having to meet anyone except the kindly car driver.

By the time they were settled into the unit and had finished a rough and ready meal, he was bushed and ready for bed.

His bravado and determination to be independent didn't last too long. Ann pointed out that whilst she might be naïve in terms of lovemaking, she had spent a good deal of her young life caring for, and cleaning up after, patients. Not only was she familiar with the male form, she had also spent a good deal of time looking after Vincent!

The nursing instinct in her soon took over from the pride in him and he allowed her to help him with the more basic hygiene problems of being paraplegic.

Within minutes of finally being tucked up in bed, he was asleep, exhausted with the stress and activity of the day.

'What a way to spend a 'honeymoon' night,' the dedicated young nurse thought to herself as she cleaned and tidied up before slipping into her plain soft-cotton nightdress and sliding into bed quietly, so as not to wake her man.

She lay there for quite some time, listening to Vince's breathing